Dear Parent:
Your child's love of readin[

Every child learns to read in a different wa~~y and a~~
speed. Some go back and forth between reading levels and read
favorite books again and again. Others read through each level in
order. You can help your young reader improve and become more
confident by encouraging his or her own interests and abilities. From
books your child reads with you to the first books he or she reads
alone, there are I Can Read Books for every stage of reading:

SHARED READING
Basic language, word repetition, and whimsical illustrations,
ideal for sharing with your emergent reader

BEGINNING READING
Short sentences, familiar words, and simple concepts
for children eager to read on their own

READING WITH HELP
Engaging stories, longer sentences, and language play
for developing readers

READING ALONE
Complex plots, challenging vocabulary, and high-interest topics
for the independent reader

I Can Read Books have introduced children to the joy of reading
since 1957. Featuring award-winning authors and illustrators and a
fabulous cast of beloved characters, I Can Read Books set the
standard for beginning readers.

A lifetime of discovery begins with the magical words "I Can Read!"

Visit www.icanread.com for information
on enriching your child's reading experience.

The One and Only Ivan: New Friends
Copyright © 2020 Disney

www.icanread.com

ISBN 978-0-06-301709-2

20 21 22 23 24 LSCC 10 9 8 7 6 5 4 3 2 1 ❖ First Edition

I Can Read!

Disney
The One And Only IVAN
New Friends

by Colin Hosten
Illustrated by Disney Storybook Art Team
Screenplay by Mike White

HARPER
An Imprint of HarperCollinsPublishers

Hi, I'm Ivan.

I'm a silverback gorilla.

That's me on the sign!

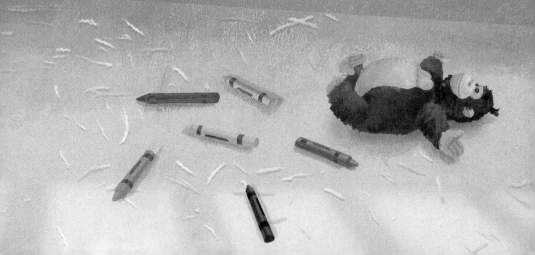

Murphy

Henrietta

Thelma

My friends and I
perform together.

Frankie

Bob

This is Ruby.

She is a little elephant.

Ruby just joined the show.

We are part of a circus.

People come to watch us perform.

It's a big job!

Ruby is a little nervous.

But I tell her not to worry.

I hope this makes Ruby feel better.

I draw pictures
to make Ruby feel happy.
She likes my drawings.

Ruby wants to draw, too!
But Ruby doesn't know
what to draw.

I tell Ruby not to worry!

She can draw whatever she wants!

I give Ruby crayons.

She has many colors

to choose from!

But where is the gray?

It's missing!

I help Ruby look for the missing crayon.

Ah! I found it.

Here is the gray crayon!

Now Ruby can

draw her picture.

Ruby draws a picture of an elephant.

Ruby also draws a picture of a gorilla.

Look!

That's a picture of me and her!

Uh-oh.

What about the rest

of our friends?

I will draw them!

How many friends do I have to draw?

I will need to count.

We have so many friends!

I try to count them.

One, two, three, four?

"Bob, can you help me count?"

But Bob is not very good at math.

Bob is a dog.

My new friend Ruby helps me count.

Now I know how many to draw.

We did it!

Ruby meets my friends.

Now we're all friends!

Now Ruby isn't nervo

It's showtime!